Usborne

Little Children's Unicorns Pad

Written by Kirsteen Robson

Designed by Jenny Brown

Illustrated by Penny Bell, Manola Caprini,
Jordan Wray, Maria Neradova, Jenny Winstanley,
Dotty Lottie, Emma Haines, Cory Reid
and Lindsey Sagar

Find and circle these things in the big picture.

Draw a line along the path that has the most rainbows.

Draw lines between three
pairs of matching pictures.

Spot 3 differences.

Draw around the unicorn
that matches this shape.

Follow the trails to see which
unicorn will fly to the hilltop.

Lucky

Valentina

Starshine

Find and circle...

...three fairies

...a dragon

...a rabbit
with wings

...and a green troll.

Trace over the dotted lines
to finish the unicorn.

Circle the view below that Breeze can see.

Breeze

A

B

C

Circle the unicorn that is flying the wrong way.

Draw more spots, so that
each unicorn has five.

Fill in all the shapes that have green dots.
What do you see?

13

Find and circle...

...a frog

...three
birds

...two blue
unicorns

...and five
dragonflies.

Which trail will lead
Astara to the palace?

Astara

Connect the dots in number order.

Spot 3 differences.

Draw wings on the flying unicorns that need them.

Find and circle all the letters in the word...
star

Find the hidden words. They may be written across or down. One has been found for you.

a	i	m	r	i	l	s
t	m	a	g	i	c	w
a	t	n	g	n	a	i
i	s	e	h	o	r	n
l	o	o	h	i	a	g
o	i	h	o	o	f	s
a	s	h	a	n	a	a

tail ✓   hoofs
horn   wings
mane   magic

Circle the cookie that does not match any other.

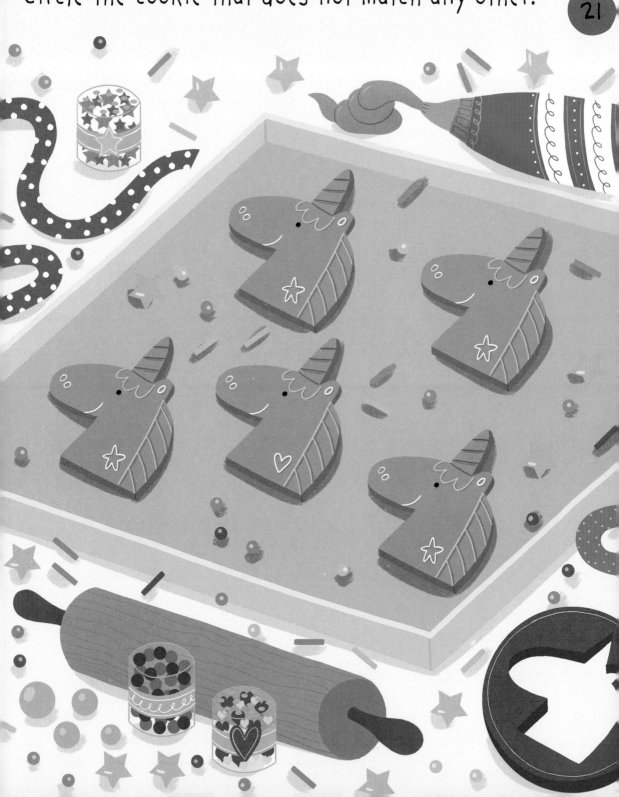

Circle the crayon that was not
used to fill in the picture.

Draw a line to show Starfrost the way across the icy water.

Starfrost

Copy the pattern of each baby unicorn's blanket onto its mother's blanket.

Circle the princess who is
holding Spectra's rope.

Spectra

Draw around these two groups in the picture below.

1.

2.

Spot 3 differences.

Connect the dots in number order.

29

Lead Sunbeam along the path with the fewest elves.

Sunbeam

Draw a line between each pair
of matching creatures.

Lead Rainbow Drop along the road to the carriage stop.

Rainbow Drop

STOP

Circle Velvetina's picture.

She has a
blue mane...

...a yellow horn...

...a red flower
behind her ear...

...and a star-shaped
neck charm.

Draw a line between each
unicorn and his baby.

Are there more suns or rainbows?

Find and circle...

...three rabbits

...two owls

...six fireflies

...and five
unicorns.

Draw a line to lead Gemma along the path with the most crystals.

Gemma

Spot 3 differences.

Write 1, 2, 3 or 4 on each picture to put the seasons in order. Start with Spring.

Circle the unicorn that does not match any other.

Lead Perdita along the path to the mountains.

Perdita

Find and circle these things in the big picture.

Draw on the parts that are missing from each unicorn so each has a horn, wings and a tail.

Fill in all the shapes that have pink dots.
What do you see?

Follow the trails to see which unicorn will go to the palace.

Rosalie

Flavia

Bianca

Circle the piece that will finish the picture.

Circle Sparkle's home.

It has a yellow flag...

...a blue
door...

...and green stripes.

Sparkle

Draw a line to lead Timera along the path with the fewest snow monsters.

Timera

Circle the winner of the cake competition.

It has pink icing...

...a blue horn

...and two layers.

Which path will lead Posie Prancer to the carriage?

Posie Prancer

Find and circle...

...a monster in a swamp

...two birds

...a rainbow

...a snowman

...and a mermaid.

Find and circle all the letters in the word...
cloud

Spot 5 differences.

Are there enough gems to put five in each basket?

Are there more unicorns
with wings or without?

Draw around these two groups in the picture below.

1.

2.

Lead Lilac along the path to Berry Dancer.

Lilac

Berry Dancer

Find the hidden words. They may be written across or down. One has been found for you.

o	e	o	e	b	r	r
p	u	r	p	l	e	e
n	r	a	y	u	d	a
e	u	n	n	e	e	d
r	l	g	r	e	e	n
l	y	e	l	l	o	w
l	e	l	n	d	u	n

red ✓   purple

blue   orange

green   yellow

Draw a line between each unicorn and
the fairy wearing clothes that match it.

Circle the unicorn that is facing the wrong way.

The patterns on the flags are in a sequence.
Will flag A, B or C be next?

A

C

B

Answer: ....

Circle the unicorn that is
not one of a matching pair.

Lead Silkentail along the path to
the enchanted cave.

Silkentail

Connect each set of
dots in number order.

1 2 3 7

1 2 3 4

1 2 3 4 5 6

4 5 6 7 8

Find and circle...

...five unicorns inside the palace

...six yellow flowers

...three flags

...and ten birds.

Circle the piece that will finish the picture.

Circle the object that is not
one of a matching pair.

MAGICAL GIFTS

I ♥ UNICORNS

I ♥ UNICORNS

Use the clues to find Starlet, winner of the Unicorn of the Year Show.

She is standing still.

Her tail has a bow.

Her blanket is pink.

Circle three things that you would need to dress up as a flying unicorn.

Lead Saltarella along the path to the jungle temple.

Saltarella

Find and circle...
...5 hares

...2 eagles

...and 3 yellow unicorns.

Draw a line along the rainbow path
without touching the edges.

Spot 5 differences.

Find the hidden words. They may be written across or down. One has been found for you.

```
o  s  l  y  e  s  e
s  k  f  o  w  s  s
e  y  i  d  l  k  w
t (s  e  a) e  a  o
h  i  l  l  s  s  o
w  d  d  a  d  y  d
d  e  s  e  r  t  s
```

sea ✓   woods
sky   fields
hills   deserts

Circle the piece that will finish the picture.

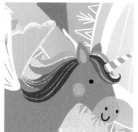

Draw around these two groups in the picture below.

1.

2.

Draw around the flying unicorn that matches this shape.

Lead the Unicorn Express to the passengers at the station.

Are there more blue
or purple unicorns?

Lead Tippletoes safely across the stepping stones to the other side of the river.

Tippletoes

Circle the cupcake that is not one of a matching pair.

Draw a line along the path to the finish without touching its edges.

Each carriage picks up one person.
How many people will be left waiting?

Answer: ....

WAIT
HERE

Draw a line along the path Glitterwings should take to reach the Three Peaks.

Glitterwings

Three Peaks

Spot 6 differences.

Lead Petula through the flower gardens to her friends.

Petula

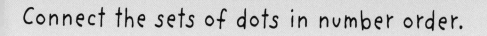

1 2 3

6 7 10 1 4 5

4 5 8 9 2 3 6 7

8 9 10 11 12

Lead Estella along the path to her tower.

Estella

Answers

1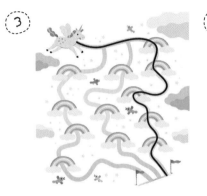

4

7

2

5

8

3

6

10 Answer: C

Answers

11

14

19

15

20

12

16

21

13

17

22

20

a	i	m	r	i	l	s
t	m	a	g	i	c	w
a	t	n	g	n	a	i
i	s	e	h	o	r	n
l	o	o	h	i	a	g
o	i	h	o	o	f	s
a	s	h	a	n	a	a

Answers

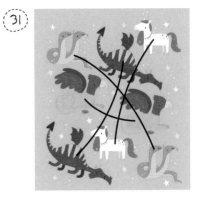

(23)

(28)

(31)

(25)

(29)

(32)

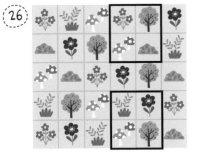

(26)

(30)

(33)

(27)

Answers

 34

 38

 42

35 There are more rainbows.

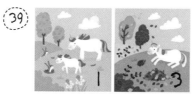 39

43

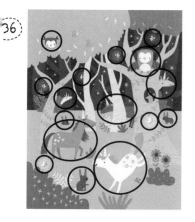 36

 40

44 There are more white stars.

 37

 41

 46

Answers

47

50

53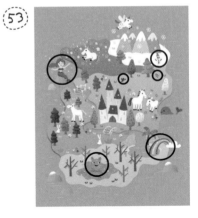

48

51

54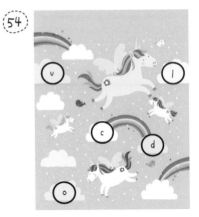

49

52

55

56 Answer: Yes

57 There are more unicorns without wing.

Answers

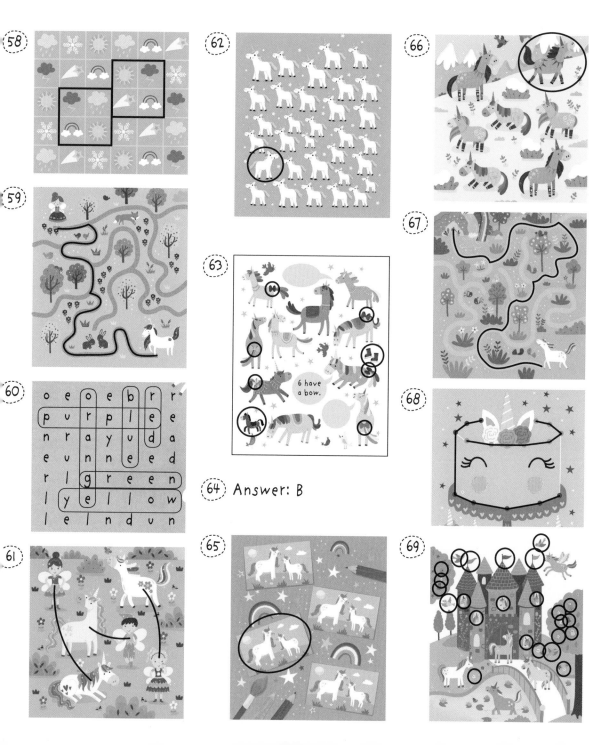

64 Answer: B

Answers

70

71

72

73

74

75

77

78

o	s	l	y	e	s	e
s	k	y	f	o	w	s	s
e	y	f	i	d	l	k	w
t		s	e	a	e	a	o
h	i	l	l	s			o
w	d	d	a	d	y	d
d	e	s	e	r	t	s	s

79

80

81